SHE FELL IN LOVE WITH HER BEST FRIEND

SHARAD RAJ C

ISBN 979-8885569553-4

Contents

I thank Scribbled thoughts for agreeing to be the fiction partner for my book. Scribbled thoughts is one of a kind platform for all budding writers, with heart touching content. I personally have been a part of the journey of Scribbled thoughts and I believe it's going to make it big someday.

Love,
Sharad

1

It was a cold winter night, and the windows were all closed. She wrapped herself in the blanket and kept staring at the phone screen for his message. She smiled a little wide looking at his text. And at once she was lost in her world of his. She knew she had started feeling something different for him, she wanted to tell him but she was afraid that letting out her feelings would affect their friendship. She wasn't sure if it was love, but that feeling of holding his hands for the rest of her life, those butterflies in her stomach she would get when she would see him, that feeling which she wasn't able to describe, was definitely not just friendship, she knew.

She wanted to tell him her feelings, she wanted to tell him how she had started feeling something different for him, how she only wanted him in this world of so many people. But at the same time she was afraid that *what if he didn't feel the same.* She didn't want to lose their friendship which meant the world to her. She was lost in the pool of thoughts, and didn't know what to do. She at once picked up her phone and dialed her friend.

'Hello.'

'Hi Meeta, did you sleep?'

'No, I was chanting mantras.'

'Haha, really?'

'Common Mithali, it's 1AM in the night, what else will I do without sleeping.'

'Okay, listen na, I was thinking of telling Arnav about my feelings.'

'Yeah, then tell this to me again for the 100th time again on some random night, that too by disturbing my sleep.'

'No this time I am sure, I have made up my mind.'

'Okay Mithali, good, wake me up when that happens, now let me sleep,' Meeta said, in a drowsy tone.

"I was just thinking if you could give me some advice, you know," Mithali softly said.

'Oh god! This girl! Kill me! Please kill me! I already gave you a lot of advice till now girl, just follow them.'

'Maybe you could, you know, give me some advice again.'

'Oh god! Fine! So don't think so much about what might happen or what might not happen okay, just say what you feel, just let it out, it doesn't have to be perfect, just tell him you love him.'

'Ah! I am just scared, I don't want the bond we share to change you know, I don't know it might creep him out, or he might start avoiding me, I just don't know.'

'The bond might change Mithali, but that doesn't mean that you stop yourself from expressing how you feel, you should never hide something which is true. Or maybe, just maybe, who knows, he might feel the same too.'

'Hmm,' Mithali said, after a pause.

'I know all this will not happen, we had this conversation infinite times, now can I please sleep?'

'Oh darling! You are so sweet! You picked up my call even when you were asleep, will you be mine? Can I marry you?'

'I am not gonna melt cutiepie, now please let me sleep, I am really sleepy re.'

'Haha, okay! You may sleep my lord! Good night!'

As soon as she said good night, the call ended. Mithali knew that Meeta was very sleepy yet she had lifted her call and spoke to her. She felt happy that she had her, she smiled looking at her name, and was lost thinking about how she had met her the first day of college and how they went from friends to close friends to best friends to family. Meeta felt like family. She was the one whom Mithali would share everything with. Be it an Ex messaging her or be it seeing a cat on her way to college, she would end up sharing everything with Meeta. And Meeta would listen to her patiently without cutting her off, cracking jokes in the middle, laughing at her but also hyping her at the same time. They were each other's biggest support system.

Mithali didn't know how she had slowly drifted away from Meeta, and started thinking about Arnav now. She was lost thinking about how she had first met him and all the memories they made together. Suddenly out of nowhere something struck her mind. She at once got up from her bed and started looking around her room for a diary. She knew she had hidden it somewhere in her room last time but she didn't remember where. It had been months now since she had opened that diary, she tried hard to recollect where she had kept the diary but she remembered nothing. After minutes of searching and trying to recollect where she had kept the diary, she had finally found it; a black leather diary with 2017 inscribed on it.

2

Mithali opened the diary and started reading through the first few pages of the diary..*Perfection.. Everyone is way too obsessed with being perfect. Be it the way they look or walk or dress, they just want to match up to perfection. But have they ever thought that in the process of being perfect, they end up losing a part of themselves little by little.. I feel perfection isn't attractive, because it is that touch of imperfection that adds wildness to the soul! Oh! It is that imperfection which makes you stand out from others, in the world full of people trying to be perfect, be that imperfect soul.* "Wow! Impressive," Mithali thought, as she went on to read the next few pages. She kept reading the pages in the very beginning and she skipped a few pages after that and then again something caught her eye..

I am so proud of myself, I never thought I would get a seat in NID, like seriously! National Institute of design! I am really happy, maybe this isn't so big, maybe it's just a college, but sometimes the little achievements matter too! For me they matter a lot! It's these little achievements that give you the boost to achieve something big. I don't know what I'll do next, I don't know what might suddenly start to interest me, but I know that I'll do only what makes me happy. It's going to be my first day tomorrow. I am excited but also a little nervous. Mithali turned the page and started to read about her first day in college.

Dear diary,

I am so excited to write about my day today in college. What happened was I was running a little late to college even on the first day haha! So I entered the college and I asked the details for my first class near the main block, then as I was making my way upstairs to the class, there was another guy who was making his way upstairs too! We smiled looking at each other! Turns out, he's my classmate. We are from the same class. We sat together and Introduced each other. His name is Arnav. We were with each other for the rest of the day. We went to classes together, we had lunch together, we sat on the same bench, and we talked a lot. He seemed to be a nice guy and had a smiling face all throughout. He's kind of cute too and smelled well. And guess what, he reads novels too! We had many things in common! Like really, his favourite colour was black too and he loves having coffee and he loves dogs. Oh! I seemed to make a friend, not quite sure yet but I can say I think he'll be my good friend in the coming days. And oh ya! The campus was great! The teachers seemed kind of okay and the canteen had nice food. I seemed to like the college, maybe because I found a stranger who accompanied me or maybe because the college was nice,

I don't know. And also you know what? We exchanged numbers in the end. He said he will call me if he doesn't find me in college tomorrow. Oh! I could figure out he just wanted my number, because he was giving lame reasons, but it's okay, he seemed to be a nice guy! Now bye dear diary, we'll meet again tomorrow maybe.. I'll keep you updated.

Mithali kept reading the next few pages as old memories flashed back. She felt a sigh of relief that she didn't miss writing the diary here and there. It had everything written down, right from day 1 to day 7. Most of it was about Arnav. She had written about what they had talked, what they had discussed, how they had met new people, how they never stopped going to classes together and how they became a little closer everyday.

Mithali felt good reading through all the diary entries. She at once wanted to call Arnav and talk to him, but she knew it was already too late. She went on to read the next few pages lightly until something caught her eye..

"Our first fight"
I am so sad today, I never thought Arnavcould do this to me, like why did he even do that, I am not short, or maybe I am not so short! Maybe I am just a little short, but that doesn't mean that he calls me 'Shortie!' What kind of a name is that? I have such a nice name, Mithali.. He could nicely call me by my name, but no, he suddenly wants to tease me by all weird

names. I ended up shouting at him, I am not gonna keep quiet if he simply calls me by weird nicknames. Like, common dude! My parents didn't give me names just to be called by such stupid nicknames. Ugh! I hate this. Now he's acting as if it's not his mistake. He didn't even text me till now, he has started ignoring me.. I don't know what to do. But I am not gonna say sorry! It was his mistake, and if he wouldn't have called me by that stupid nickname, I wouldn't have shouted at him. Ugh! It's just so frustrating, when people commit a mistake and they act as if it was not their mistake at all. Anyways, let's see what happens! I hate it that he's the only close friend I made in college. Now I am gonna stop writing and sleep! Let's meet some other day.

"Haha, this is so funny and stupid, I could have just teased him too instead of shouting, thank god that he handled it nicely," Mithali smiled, turning the page. She skipped a few pages after that and was almost half way through the diary and suddenly the title of a particular page felt Intriguing. "Our day together at home."

3

Maybe with some people you just have that comfort zone, maybe you just have that trust. With some people you just know, it feels right, you know that that person will do no harm to you no matter what. Arnav feels right. With him around I feel safe, he knows how to make me laugh and smile, he takes care of me like I matter and never makes me feel alone in his presence. I never knew that I would get this attached with Arnav, maybe he didn't know too that he'll get that attached to me. It feels nice to spend time with him, okay wait! All I am trying to say is, my parents weren't home yesterday, I was all alone at home and I was so bored. I called Arnav and asked him to come over to my place. It was so beautiful, I will never forget that day. First we sat and we talked for so long, and then we played cards, we had so much fun and then we cooked together, we made food, we had lunch together and then we watched a movie together. It was so soothing, maybe that's how it feels to spend time with your best friend all alone. And then at night he had dinner and he left. I don't have words to describe how it felt, It's a moment that I will remember always and forever.

As she read through the words, Mithali could exactly feel how it felt back then. She remembered all the conversations they had, word to word. She remembered how he had cheated while playing the game of cards. Mithali smiled a little wider as old memories flashed back. She read through more pages and Imagined every moment she had spent with him. She was lost thinking about him and wished for him to be there at the moment. She kept reading the diary, skipping through a few pages and reading a few and as she was turning the pages she found yet another Interesting title.

"13 good things about Arnav."

1) He never judges no matter what, you can say the most random thing yet he will react in a very cool way saying it's normal, maybe I have never met someone like him before who doesn't at all judge.

2) He is a very kind soul, he's always there to help no matter what, and no matter whether someone is good or bad to him, he is always kind.

3) He treats everyone the same, poor - rich, Toppers - back benchers, almost everyone. He treats all of them equally. He has friends everywhere.

4) If he wants to do something, he believes in himself and it doesn't matter to him what others say or think about him.

5) He is very Intelligent.

6) He has a soft heart and cares for everyone, he cares even for people who don't care for him. Sometimes It's toxic, but sometimes it awes me how he has such a good heart and has a pure soul.

7) He doesn't cheat and keeps his promises. Once he promises something, we can count on it, and no matter how easy or hard it is, if he promises he will do it.

8) He never breaks trust.

9) He makes people feel comfortable around him, he doesn't act as if he's the only one who knows everything.

10) He encourages people to do better, he supports them, he gets the best out of people.

11) He values people's feelings.

12) He stands by what is correct, and doesn't tolerate wrong.

13) He is cute.

"When on earth did I even write this lol, this is so cheesy and oops! Did I fall for him way before I knew it?" Mithali laughed. *Should hide this book in a safer place as soon as I finish reading,* she thought, going on to read the last few pages of the diary. It was 4AM already and here she was, recollecting all the memories that she had with him. Part of her wanted to confess her feelings for him, part of her was afraid that she might end up losing him. After a few minutes she got up from bed and hid the diary in a safe place. This time she made a note of where she was hiding the diary so she could find it easily the next time.

She switched off the lights and laid there on the bed.She kept thinking if she should confess her feelings. Even though she was afraid, she knew this was something she had to tell him. After so much of over thinking, after all the if's and maybes, after all the pros and cons, she finally made up her mind that she's going to tell him tomorrow, that she can't hide something which is real.

She checked her phone and kept it away. She tried sleeping. She wanted the night to end already. She wanted to see him. She was excited and at the same time afraid of the next day. She had decided she was going to finally let out her feelings, something which was true, something which she meant from all her heart. But was she about to lose her friendship?

4

'I love you Arnav, you mean the world to me. I don't know when but I have fallen for you so badly. I don't know if you feel the same, but I just wanted to tell you how I feel. I have been hiding it for a few months now but it's killing me inside everyday so I just wanted to let my feelings out. Do you love me too, Arnav?'

'Mithali, I don't know, it's just that. . . .'

This is a modern fairytale, no happy endings.... the song kept playing. And with a jerk she woke up from her sleep. Her phone was still ringing, she slowly reached out for the phone and picked the call. It was Arnav.

'Good morning lazy ass, you are coming to college today right?' Arnav asked.

'No, I ain't coming.'

'Fine, I won't go too!'

'I was kidding, I am going to college.'

'Then get up quick and get ready, I am already in college waiting for you.'

'You told you won't go if I don't go, how come you went already?' Mithali laughed.

'Well, I knew you'd come for me, if I asked you to, so I went.'

'Smooth! Fine, see you In college.'

'Yeah! And hey, I am sorry if I disturbed you from your sleep.'

'This is no new, this has become routine now,' she laughed.

When the call ended, Mithali quickly got up and sat on bed. She had only 3hours of sleep and it felt difficult for her to leave the bed. After a few minutes she somehow got up from bed to get ready.

While she was getting ready she was thinking about the dream she had. She didn't know if confessing her feelings was the right thing to do but she wanted to do it anyway.

She drove fast and In about twenty minutes she reached the college. She wanted to see Arnav, meet him, spend time with him, and hold his hand. Moreover, whenever Arnav told her he was waiting for her she made sure she reached faster. Such was her love for him. She cared about his feelings, she didn't do things which would make him feel bad, she never kept him waiting for so long, and even cared about those little little things about him.

On seeing her parking the scooty, Arnav went closer to her and hugged her. They talked with each other and together they walked to their favourite spot in the college. They settled under the trees and started talking again. She was lost in his eyes and his voice felt so soothing. She wanted to be with him for the rest of life, he was her home, and she wanted to be in it.

'Mithali, are you even listening to me?'

'Umm, yeah!tell me I am listening', Mithali said, coming back to senses.

'So I was saying, I have started dating a girl.'

'Oh wow! When did that happen?' Mithali asked, trying to make sense of what he had just said, feeling all weak.

'Well it.....' Arnav's phone started ringing before he could complete the sentence.

'Just give me a minute Mithali, I'll answer this call and come back,' Arnav said, getting up from where he was sitting.

While Arnav was gone, Mithali felt weak. She didn't want to be there. She wanted to just go home and let her tears out. It felt as if her world had collapsed. Her eyes were watery and seeing Arnav coming back to her. She gently wiped her tears and smiled looking at Arnav, trying to hide her pain.

Sitting beside Mithali, Arnav said, 'So do you know what her name is?

'Who? The one you have started dating?'

'Yes.'

"No, I don't know, tell me what her name is.'

'It's Mithali.'

'What? Were you joking when you said you started dating?'

'What do you think?'

'I don't know Arnav, you tell me.'

'Her name is definitely not Mithali, that was just to test if you were listening,' Arnav laughed.

'So what's her name?'

'Her name is Khushi.'

'Umm... nice.'

While Arnav was explaining the details of how it started. Mithali was feeling the pain building in her. She knew she would begin crying if she listened to more of what Arnav was saying. 'Hey Arnav, listen!',Mithali said at once.

'That girl over there has been looking at you since so long.'

With that, Arnav looked back and started laughing. Their talks continued for sometime and then they got up to attend classes.

Finally when the college was done, Mithali left college soon, telling Arnav that she had some urgent work to do. On her way home she couldn't stop thinking about what had happened. She wanted him more than a best friend, she wanted to hold his hand, hug him, listen to his heartbeat and be there for him not just as his best friend but as his partner, as his girlfriend, as his soulmate. She tried to control her tears but they wouldn't stop. Just to make it better, all at once it started raining. Tears rolled down her eyes as she cried with every inch of her soul. The rain hid her tears and all through her way home, she kept crying.

5

As soon as Mithali reached home, she went to her room and changed her clothes. She wiped her body with a towel, got fresh and wore new clothes. She sat on her bed thinking of Arnav. She was done crying, she knew now that he was dating someone else but at least he was still her best friend, that made her feel better.

She took her phone at once and called Meeta.

'Hellooo Lady!'Meeta sounded all excited.

'You seem to be in a certain kind of mood,' Mithali teased.

'Oh ya! You called me right so I am in a certain kind of mood.'

'Haha, common! Tell me the truth Meeta.'

'I am happy because my parents finally agreed to get a dog.'

'Wow! Wow! Wow! I am coming to your home everyday okay? Whenever you get a dog.'

'Yes you can, only if you agree to get me a Pizza everytime you come,' Meeta laughed.

'Better I kidnap your dog instead,' Mithali laughed.

'Yes, only if your parents allow you to keep the dog at home,' Meeta teased.

'Yeah, that's there. No problem, I'll still kidnap, I can hide it in my room.'

'Oh no! You can't! Again if your mom finds out she'll be like Mithali beta, what is this! I didn't expect this from you. You are grown up now, you cannot be irresponsible like this..'Meeta laughed.

'Dude! I just wish even your parents were as strict as mine.'

'Oh lady! Shh! Go away! Don't wish that.'

And with that both laughed at once. After a little pause, Meeta continued..

'So someone was telling me at night that they will be doing something today, where did that come till?'

'Just don't ask about it dude! It all got fucked up.'

'Shit! Tell me what happened Mithali.'

'Nothing, I made up my mind that I am going to tell him my feelings anyway, we were even alone for sometime, I was even about to say.. But just then.. '

'Then what.. Will you please stop giving that pause, just say it.'

'The point is, he's starting dating someone else, and her name is Khushi.'

After a long pause, with a soft tone, Meeta asked, 'How are you doing Mithali?'

'I don't know Meeta, I had imagined going on a date with him for so long, not just going out together but going on a proper date, where we would hold each other's hand, talk, and you know maybe kiss.

Now he might be doing all this with someone else, and knowing that that someone isn't me, it hurts. I cried on my way back home, I don't know, I just want him.'

'Want me to come home?' Meeta asked.

'No, I guess I'll be fine. Just a matter of time.'

'Maybe you should listen to the fisherman story.'

'And what's that?'

'Do you want me to tell you the story?'

'Yes please do, but Meeta please don't tell me any lame story okay, trust me, I'll just kill you if you do that right now.'

'Haha, I don't know if it's lame but just listen to this.'

'Yeah go on...'

'So, there was once a fisherman in the village who used to catch fishes everyday, made money from selling them and then provided food and shelter for his family with the money. Once what happened was, the fisherman found a golden fish, the fish was so adorable that he decided to save it and take it to his home. He then built a small pond near his home and let the fish stay in the pond. She had become a part of his family. He used to feed the fish everyday and used to stay with the fish everyday whenever he was sad..'

'Wait! I am sorry for cutting you off, but how did he know that it was a she?' Mithali laughed.

'Common! That's not the point, listen silently.'

'Okay!'

'Like that the fish had become very close to him, one day what happened was the fish died. He was very upset, he was angry that the fish died. And then for days he cried, and didn't go fishing again. But he had to go fishing because that's how he got money. So he somehow got up and after a few days started fishing again. After a few days what happened was, he found a silverfish, more adorable than the golden one. That's how life is, we get so stuck with one person that we stop looking for other people. We forget that there are many fishes in the pond. Maybe that person was very dear to us, maybe we loved that person so deeply, maybe there's no one else like that person, but that's okay! We will find another fish again someday when we are ready for fishing. Because life will give you so many opportunities, just because you lost one doesn't mean that there are no opportunities left.'

'That was nice Meeta, thank you! Now I know why you are always ready for fishing,' Mithali teased.

'Haha, stop! Take care okay! I won't tell you it's going to be fine, but I am here, we can spend time together, go out, do things together. Just call me up whenever you are low.'

'That's so sweet Meeta, I don't know what I would have done without you.'

'Haha! Stop buttering. It's been 2 hours since we were on call, now we'll end the call? I'll go for a walk.'

'Okay Meeta, will call you back again.'

As the call ended Mithali was feeling better than before. She instantly knew that she's going to be fine in a few days and that it's just a phase. Just when she was thinking about all that Meeta had said, her phone rang. It was Arnav.

'Hello!' She answered the call in a good tone.

'Mithali, I texted you an address, get ready and come to the address I sent'

'What? It's 7PM now Arnav, the location seems to be very far from my place, why do you want me to come?'

'I know It's 7, but I really want you to come. There's a surprise for you, now get up and move your lazy ass, come as soon as possible.'don't be late!'

'Ah! Fine! I'll kill you if there's no surprise.'

'Trust me, there is a surprise for you. Now come soon.'

'Okay fine, now let me get ready, bye!'

'Yeah.'

As soon as the call ended, Mithali laid flat on the bed. *Oh god!* She thought. She wanted to take a nap, but after all her best friend had called her out and she couldn't say no. She then swiftly got up from her bed to get ready.

6

In about half an hour Mithali reached the place he had asked her to come. It was very far from her home yet she drove as fast as possible so she could make it to the place early. On reaching, she saw Arnav waiting for her outside.

'Hey!' she said, seeing him.

Parking the scooty to the side she went closer to him and hugged him.

'So, what's the surprise?',Mithali asked.

'The surprise is right here,' Arnav said as he pulled a beautiful girl from beside. Mithali hadn't even noticed she had been there with him.

'Meet her, she's khushi.' Arnav said.

'Hey Khushi! You look beautiful! I am Mithali, Arnav's friend,' she said, shaking her hand.

'Thanks Mithali, Arnav tells me a lot about you,' Khushi replied.

'Oh wow! Thank you Arnav! I must say you are very lucky that you got him. He's a very nice person,' Mithali said.

'You are nice too Mithali,' Khushi smiled.

'Thank you Khushi, you are very sweet,' Mithali smiled back, as the three made their way inside the restaurant.

The talks continued... Mithali felt nice talking to her. She had those positive vibes that made everyone around her comfortable. She was almost like Arnav; nice, sweet and beautiful. But she'd feel jealous whenever she saw them both holding hands. At one end Mithali was happy that her best friend is finally not single and has found someone beautiful. And at the other end she was sad that she wouldn't get the same attention anymore.

The evening passed by with all the three sharing stories.Khushi talked about her goals and dreams and shared some of her childhood memories while Arnav and Mithali talked about how they had met and how they ended up being best friends. The moment felt nice and time seemed to just fly by..

The stars started to shine bright. The sky was dark and the clock went 10 'o' clock. It was then that they finally decided to leave. While going home, Mithali cursed everything that was happening. She wanted him but he was already dating. She knew, if she carried this feeling for a little longer it would burn her up into ashes. She smiled instead, pretending nothing had happened. *There's nothing like you will always get what you want, and if he loves someone else it's really fine, I am there for myself,* she calmed herself.

* * *

On reaching home, her notification tone rang. It was Arnav's message.

And looking at the message, she smiled a little wide.

'Monkey! Text me when you reach home. Just so that I know you reached home safely.' Arnav's text read.

'Reached just now!' She texted back and went to bed. As soon as she texted he replied back in a second. 'Thanks for coming, It really felt nice that you came.'

'I felt nice too Monkey!' She texted back.

'By the way, how was Khushi, do you think I should date her?'

Looking at his message, part of her wanted to say*no idiot! date me! I love you.* But she knew that that's not how she should reply.

'She looks good, she's cute and nice, and if you feel nice being with her, if you want to spend time with her, you should.'

'Haha, thank you! We'll find you a boyfriend soon! Don't worry!'

She wanted to say that he was the one whom she wanted as her boyfriend, that he's the one whom she imagines spending time with but she just couldn't say.

'First concentrate on your girlfriend or she'll simply leave you,' Mithali teased him.

'You are more important than her so we are getting you a boyfriend okay?'

'Oh god! Fine! Now let me sleep?'

'Oh yes! Bye!'

'By the way, you reached home safely right?'
'Yes, I did.'
'What about Khushi?'
'She did too.'
'Alright, I'll sleep then, bye!'
'Bye.'
Imagining him with Khushi, she was feeling low already, tears rolled down her eyes with the thought that her best friend didn't fall in love with her like she had fallen. *It's okay Mithali, it's fine,* she told herself while she cried more. The night seemed long and she kept crying and crying until she finally fell asleep.

7

Few months had passed by since Arnav had started dating Khushi. Times had changed. The connection, the bond, between Mithali and Arnav wasn't the same. In the first month of Arnav dating Khushi, everything seemed to be fine. He shared everything with Mithali, they went together to places, they would crack jokes, talk on video calls, and call each other everyday. But things got worse in the second month. Arnav would not meet Mithali all the time, they would not hang out often, and in college spending time with each other for hours together changed to spending time with each other for minutes. All it took was one month of dating to change a bond so deep. Mithali knew that everything was changing but she wanted to give Arnav that space. She knew that that's how relationships work, you have to give time to your partner. And Arnav not giving time to her was okay with her, because she knew that he was dating someone and he needed to give time to the girl he was dating.

She believed that if she and Arnav were meant to be together they would end up being together. Yet, sometimes it would hurt her so badly and she would end up crying for him, but she knew that nothing can be done now as he was already dating someone else.

In these two months Mithali had started going to dance classes. She kept doing new things, focused on academics, and read novels. She did everything that would keep her busy, because she knew that the moment she was free she would end up thinking about Arnav and start crying.

On a hot Tuesday afternoon, Mithali made her way to the dance class. She was running late already and she rushed through the main gate. And just then to her surprise she saw Khushi. They both exchanged glances.

'Hey, hi Mithali,' Khushi said, coming closer to her.

'Hi Khushi,' Mithali shook her hand.

'How are you doing? It's been a long time since I have seen you.'

'I am fine Khushi, how are you?'

'I am fine too! You come here for dance classes?'

'Yes, It's almost been more than a month since I joined.'

'Wow! That's great!

'You come here too?' Mithali asked.

'Yeah, I started a month back too! And also I am glad that we met.'

'I am glad too that we met,' Mithali replied back.

They stood there and talked for a few minutes and Khushi at once said,

'Hey Mithali, want to come out with me?'

'Yeah, sure!When?'

'Now?'

'Okay, I'll get my scooty, yeah?'

'Yes I'll wait here.'

On her way, Mithali wondered why Khushi wanted to go out with her. They barely knew each other and had only met once, *or maybe she is bringing Arnav too.*

'So where are we going?' Mithali asked, parking her scooty in front of Khushi.

'Just follow me,' Khushi said, starting her activa.

In a few minutes they made their way to a restaurant nearby and ordered some food. They talked about what they had been doing recently and how life is going, till the topic changed to what series they had watched recently. As the food arrived silence prevailed between them.

'So how is the relationship going with Arnav?' Mithali asked, breaking the silence.

'We..we are not dating anymore, Mithali.'

'What..why.. When did that happen?'

'It's been more than a month since we broke up.'

'What.. but why.. Like how..' Mithali asked, not able to process what Khushi had just said.

'Arnav didn't tell you?' Khushi asked.

'No, he didn't tell me at all, I didn't know about it.'

'Then you should ask ArnavMithali.'

'Common! You are not telling me about it?'

'Go ask your best friend Mithali,' Khushi laughed.

'But I am sorry to hear that, you are doing fine right? Mithali asked, looking into Khushi's eyes.

'Yes Mithali, I am fine, thank you for asking.'

'If any day you feel low, know that you can call me Khushi.'

'Thank you Mithali, I know you might have felt weird when I asked if you want to come out with me, because we don't know each other that much, but it's just that I don't feel like going out with my friends but wanted to go out with someone, so asked you, and thank you for agreeing to come.'

'Hey Khushi, common! That's fine! I am glad that you asked me to come, and trust me I had a nice time with you, be it the first time we met or be it now, I always had a nice time with you, you are so sweet. And we can go out whenever you want okay? Know that I am here for you.'

'Thank you Mithali, and do ask Arnav why we broke up.'

Mithali wondered what she meant to say, she kept thinking if she was the reason why they broke up. Ignoring her chain of thoughts she simply nodded her head.

They talked for some more time, exchanged numbers and promised to stay in touch. As Khushi left, Mithali went back to the restaurant and sat there on the seat. Now it all made sense to her, why he was busy, why he wasn't talking to her, as she recalled everything that had happened in the past one month, it all made sense to her. *Maybe he's sad*

and doesn't feel like talking to anyone.
Mithali was concerned about Arnav, this was the first time she wasn't there for him when he needed someone. She took her phone at once and messaged Arnav.

"Hey Arnav, how are you doing? Heard that you and Khushi broke up? Why did you break up?"
She kept waiting for his reply, while she kept thinking what was the reason that they broke up.

A few hours had passed by yet there was no reply from him. Mithali kept checking her phone continuously for his one notification, but that notification tone never beeped. After a few hours Mithali opened his chat, her message was seen but not replied. She wondered why he had not replied, he never left her texts unreplied before. She kept thinking why he was ignoring her.

'Hey, are you there? Are you ignoring me?' she texted him again.

'Hey Mithali, sorry, I saw your text but forgot to reply, I am not ignoring you,' Arnav texted back after a few minutes.

'So, you and Khushi broke up?'

'Yes we did.'

'But why? What happened?'

'Nothing, just didn't work.'

'Are you sure Arnav?'

'Yes.'

'I am asking you again, are you sure?'

'Oh god! Yes Mithali, I am sure. Why did you even ask me that?'

'Arnav, maybe I might be wrong but I know that there's definitely more to it, there's definitely a reason behind it, and it's okay if you don't want to share. However maybe I am not that important to you anymore, because once I used to be that person in your life with whom you'd share everything. Be it even the little things, you used to share everything. But now you didn't even tell me that you broke up. And wow! It's been more than a month and the person who once knew every little thing happening in your life, now doesn't know anything.'

'Hey Mithali, I am sorry, there's nothing like I didn't want to tell you, it's just that I wasn't in the right space to share things, I just needed time for myself, and If it was something I wanted to tell you I would tell you. Just give me some time, I will tell you why we broke up, okay?'

'Yeah fine, I'll wait! Know that I am always there for you.'

'Thank you Mithali. By the way, who told you that me and Khushi broke up?'

'I had met Khushi today and she is the one who told me. We went out together.'

'Wow! How did you meet her and where did you people go?'

``We met at our dance class, she has joined the dance classes too. We talked for some time and from there we went to a restaurant nearby."

'Wow! You are going to dance classes now, that's great! Then didn't you ask her why we broke up?'

'I did, but she was hesitant to say. She simply asked me to ask you.'

'Okay.'

'So, why did you two break up Arnav? Are you telling me?'

'Give me some time maybe, I'll tell you.'

'Alright.'

As the chat ended, Mithali kept thinking what he was hiding. She knew that he was definitely hiding something, but had no clue what it was. As the evening slowly passed by, her phone rang, It was Arnav.

And as she lifted the call, Arnav said, 'Mithali, we need to talk.'

'Yes, tell me Arnav.'

'Not on call, let's meet.'

'Fine, let's meet at 6PM tomorrow?'

'Sure.'

'Will you at least tell me what it is about?'

'No Mithali, I want to talk to you face to face.'

'Ahh! I just hate you! You keep me in suspense all the time.'

'We will meet tomorrow, and I'll tell you okay?'

'Ugh! Fine.'

'Bye! Good night!'

'Good night.'

After the call ended Mithali wondered what it was, she kept thinking why he wanted to meet her all of a sudden. At one end she was confused as to why he wanted to meet her suddenly and at the other end she was happy that they were finally meeting, that she would finally get to see him. Whatever it was she couldn't wait for the night to end, she had mixed emotions, maybe finally all her questions were to be answered.

9

At 6PM the next day, Arnav and Mithali finally met. It was after months that they were hanging out together outside college. Mithali's soul felt happy. Maybe he didn't love her but her best friend was finally giving her some attention. They hugged each other tight as soon as they saw each other and took their seats near the corner of the coffee shop. They cracked jokes, made fun of each other and laughed with pure heart. The good old days were finally back.

Out of nowhere Arnav at once said, 'Mithali I am sorry! I have not been giving you time like I used to, is there any way you could forgive me?'

'Arnav, you know what the best part of any bond is? When you speak your heart out, when you have no ego, when you just be free, and that is what you have in you, you speak your heart out, you say sorry if you think you did anything wrong, and you do everything to make things better. I am really very happy that you are my best friend.'

'Mithali, since when did you start being so sweet.' Arnav teased.

'Since 1999,' Mithali laughed.

They continued talking again about what they had been up to in the past few days and it felt like old days again. Mithali was lost looking in his eyes. The moment felt so beautiful and she wished for the time to freeze. She wanted to hold his hand and be in his arms, she just craved for him, his presence, she craved for more moments like these with him.

'Mithali, I have a secret to share,' Arnav said, breaking her chain of imagination.

'What is it Arnav?' Mithali asked.

There was a long pause that continued. And slowly Arnav started saying, 'Mithali, I am not doing good these days. I smile, I crack jokes, I do everything normal but things aren't the same. I feel that void in my soul, there's something I can't describe. There's a piece of me that's not really happy, I don't even know how to describe it.

'Arnav, things will be fine', Mithali said, placing her hand on his.

'It's just that bad times come, but things will be okay. Now tell me exactly what happened?' She asked.

'Before I say that, tell me about you, what's going on with you?'

While he asked that, Mithali just wanted to say how she thinks of him, how she feels different for him, of how she wants to hold his hand till her last breath, of how she misses him so bad and how she cries for him.

But all she ended up saying was about her dance class, about the new people she met and about the little things.

After she finished talking, she asked, 'So what's going on with you?'

'Well Mithali, Me and Khushi aren't dating anymore.'

'God! I know that, tell me why aren't you dating? What happened all of a sudden?'

After a long silence as if trying to get his words together, Arnav finally said, 'It's because of you Mithali. Every time It's only you with whom I shared things first before sharing with anyone else. I used to call you first instead of khushi, I used to wait for your texts more than hers, I used to wait to meet you more than her, and I hadn't realised all this until Khushi told me about it. She told me it isn't my mistake and told me how it's love that I feel for you. When Khushi left I then realised that her staying or leaving never mattered. For the past one month I have been trying to tell myself that it's just friendship, but Mithaliit's love, I love you. I feared that someday we would become like those best friends who get into a relationship, be together for a few months or years and then never talk to each other again but I am willing to take the risk. And when things aren't working out between us, If I find a hundred reasons for leaving, I'll find a hundred and one reasons for holding on. I knew that maybe if you don't feel the same, our friendship would become awkward but I wasn't able to stay away from not saying this to you because I have started imagining holding your hands and walking together when we get old, I have started imagining of us together in one home, I get dreams about us hugging tight and when I wake up I feel it.'

As Arnav said all this to Mithali, tears rolled down his eyes. Mithali went close to Arnav, looked into his eyes and said, 'This moment feels like a fairytale.' He could feel those tears in her eyes too and at that moment when they held each other's hand he knew she was all he wanted in his life. Their lips spoke before words did, it all happened instantly. They looked into each other's eyes, as their lips met. They were lost in each other, they kissed till they were out of breath.

'I love you too Arnav! Trust me, I have been thinking and feeling exactly the same as you. I don't know if this will work, but I'll give my everything in it to make it work, because I want to be with you Arnav. I love you.'

As she said that, tears rolled down both their eyes and they hugged each other tighter than ever before. It felt home, safe home.

Sharad Raj C is a contemporary romance author. His books include: Scribbled Thoughts, She fell in love with her best friend, Only you, She blocked his love, To the broken and The boy who loved so deep.

Note From The Author

It means a lot to me that you have brought my book. Words will never be enough to describe how thankful I am, so I'll just say thanks even though I know that it will never be enough. I would love to hear from you. You can write to me on _sharadrajc97@gmail.com_
Or you can always connect with me on Social media. I promise I'll reply.
I wish you to be safe and know that I love you all.

Loving, breaking, and loving again. This is how life runs. You have in your hands a heart which loved so badly, Which broke so badly, Which missed so badly, which healed back so badly. You have in your hands a heart that's fragile, that would break into pieces but would not forget to attach again. Scribbled thoughts are words of loving, breaking and healing.

To the broken, is a collection of prose, poetry and musings divided into three chapters. Each chapter serves a different purpose, allowing you to feel, to heal, and to grow. This book teaches you to fall in love with yourself and to keep yourself first before others.

The boy who loved so deep, is the story about a boy who falls in love with the girl whom he first meets in college, and his phase of life.

Kaira and Vandhan, are in a relationship since long, where they are so in love with each other. Everything goes on smoothly, until Vandhan says that he wants to breakup.. what happens after that is what the story is all about.

It's been a few months since their breakup but Khushi still has feelings for her Ex. She wants him back, but she recently gets to know that her Ex has started dating someone else. She wants to text him and confess her feelings but also at the same time she wants to let go because her Ex has already moved on. Will she choose love or will she let go? Know as the time unfolds.